A Wedding to Remember

By Sara Miller
Cover and interior photography by Willy Lew, Shirley Ushirogata,
Greg Roccia, David Westphal, Steve Toth, Judy Tsuno, and Lisa Collins
Illustrations by Diane Choi

A GOLDEN BOOK • NEW YORK

BARBIE and associated trademarks are owned by and used under license from Mattel, Inc.
Copyright © 2003 Mattel, Inc. All Rights Reserved.
Published in the United States by Golden Books, an imprint of Random House Children's Books, a division of
Random House, Inc., New York, and simultaneously in Canada by Random House of Canada Limited, Toronto.
No part of this book may be reproduced or copied in any form without written permission from the copyright owner.
Golden Books, A Golden Book, and the G colophon are registered trademarks of Random House, Inc.
Library of Congress Control Number: 2002108239   www.goldenbooks.com
ISBN: 0-307-10424-9   PRINTED IN CHINA   10 9 8 7 6 5 4 3 2 1

This Diary Belongs To:

Barbie Roberts

Dear Diary,

Christie just told me the best news—**Monica is getting married!** I am so excited! But I'm also a little bit upset.

I can't believe Monica didn't tell me first. I mean, Monica is one of my oldest and best friends—we grew up together.

Hi, I'm Barbie

Hi, I'm Monica

Is she ever going to tell me?

Will I even be invited to the wedding?

Is Christie Monica's best friend now?

Monica would be one of the first people I would tell if I had **big news,** like if I was moving to Bora Bora—or if I was . . .

♥ **GETTING MARRIED!** ♥

People I would call if I had BIG NEWS

🌸 1st. My sisters (although I wouldn't have to call them because they live with me)

🌼 2nd. Monica

🍃 3rd. Midge (have to talk quickly—long-distance calls are so expensive $$$!)

🌀 4th+5th+6th. Christie, Kira, and Becky

🌊 7th. Mary

I mean, I was the one who introduced Monica and Robert. And she told Christie first????!
I don't get it. Oh, well . . .
I'll call Monica
tomorrow to
congratulate
her. YAAAAWN!
STRRRRETCHHH!
Well, good night,
Diary.

Dear Diary,

I can't tell you how bad I feel right now. I was still **mad** at Monica when I turned on my computer and saw that I had an e-mail—from MONICA! Here's why I feel as **blue** as I do:

```
Dear Barbie,
I wanted you to be the first
to hear the news. I'm getting
married! Robert just asked me
tonight and of course I said
yes. I am so happy. But that's
not all. You're my best friend
and I want you to be my maid of
honor. I don't know if I'll be
able to make it down the aisle
without your help. Please say
yes, Barbie.
          BFF (Best Friends Forever),
          Monica
```

The date of the e-mail was the very same day Monica got engaged! I can't believe it took me two days to check e-mail.

I called Monica right away to explain why I wasn't the first to congratulate her. And you know what? She wasn't even mad! She is the COOOOLEST! She was just happy that I said YES to being in her wedding. Monica wants Kelly to be her flower girl (her little brother is going to be the ring bearer—he's so cute!) and she wants Skipper to sing a solo. Monica and I are getting together to talk about THE WEDDING tomorrow morning, so I'd better get to bed. Good night, dearest Diary!

Kelly

Dear Diary,

Monica and I had fun talking about the wedding plans today. There's like a **GAZILLION** things for me to do—and **I'm not even the one getting married!**

★ Maid of Honor's Duties

☆ Help bride find perfect wedding dress
☆ Throw bridal shower
☆ Help choose flowers, cake, decorations
☆ Make sure bride has a **BLAST** on her **BIG DAY!**

Bride	Monica
Groom	Robert
Maid of Honor . . .	ME!
Best Man	Ken
Bridesmaids	Kira and Christie
Ushers	John and Steve
Flower girl	Kelly
Ring bearer	Matt

Monica already has a lot of awesome ideas for the wedding. Monica and Robert both love the outdoors, so they want to get married outside. In a park? Or maybe in a flower garden? Monica loves flowers.

Monica's faves

Oh! I almost forgot to mention that I told Skipper that Monica wanted her to sing a solo at the wedding. I thought she'd be super excited about it. Boy, was I in for a surprise. Skipper said she's too nervous to sing in front of so many people— especially people she doesn't know. What am I going to do? What will I say to Monica? I'm stumped! If only you could help me, Diary. Good night.

Dear Diary,

Today, Kira, Christie, and I took Monica shopping for dresses. We had a **BLAST!** At first, they kept bringing in all these big, puffy dresses for Monica to try on, with huge fake flowers and skirts so wide she couldn't make it out the dressing room door! We cracked up each time she came out to show us. But she finally chose one that looked **just perfect** on her.

When it was time to try on bridesmaid dresses, we all picked out the **craziest** ones in the store. Mine had a bow on the side that was bigger than my head, Kira's was the **LOUDEST, brightest shade of pink** you've ever seen, and Christie's was about five sizes **TOO BIG**—it had pins holding it up everywhere!

But in the end, Monica chose pretty **turquoise dresses** for us to wear.

At lunch, Monica told us she doesn't want our new friend Mary to feel left out because she's not in the wedding party. 🙁 I promised to think of something. **Boy!** Planning a wedding is a lot harder than I thought. Well, TTFN (ta-ta for now).

Dear Diary,

Now that **Monica and Robert have set the wedding date,** it's time to plan Monica's bridal shower. I went to the stationery store and found **the perfect invitation.** Check it out!

It's a *Bridal Shower*

For: Monica
When: Saturday, 3:00 p.m.
Where: Barbie's House

Isn't it great? But I only have two and a half weeks to plan the whole thing!

Bridal Shower List

Monica's All-Time Faves

Flavors: Coconut and strawberry

Color: Yellow

Flowers: Roses, carnations, lilies

Menu

Finger sandwiches

Cheese and crackers

Fruit salad (with lots of strawberries)

Soda

Tea

Coconut cake and strawberry ice cream

Decorations

Yellow and white flowers everywhere—
 carnations, roses

Yellow and white balloons

Streamers

Flowered plates and matching napkins

Well, I'd better say toodles because I've got

oodles to do tomorrow. Good night, Diary.

Dear Diary,

CONGRATULATIONS TO ME!
Why? you ask. Because I just ran a marathon! Okay, okay, not really. But my feet sure feel like I did. Here's why:

The Blue *Beats

Place: The Cellar
Time: 8 o'clock

We went dancing and checked out this really cool band. We must have danced for five hours straight! But each time we stopped to take a break, the band would play another great song that we just had to dance to. Monica loved them! She asked me if I thought the Blue Beats would be a good band to play at the reception. Of course I said yes (I just hope my feet recover by then).

DANCES WE DANCED

The Mashed Potato

The Twist

The Monkee

The Swim

The Funky Chicken

The Banana Peel (Monica made this up!)

How do my feet feel after tonight's dance-a-thon?

a. gr8

b. good

c. okay, I guess

d. like I just walked across 100 feet of burning hot coals

e. like a semi truck ran over them, backed up, and then ran over them again

Well, Diary. Tonight was fun, but now I'm done. It's time to put my dancing shoes away and slip on my slippers. AHHHH! Good night.

Dear Diary,

UUUGGGHHH. I don't think I'll ever be able to eat again! Why the sudden FOOD-O-PHOBIA? Well, this afternoon, I went with Monica, her mom, and Robert to the reception hall to try out all the food for the wedding. And between the four of us, I think we ate enough for a lifetime! We seriously PIGGED OUT! Everything was yummy!

★FOOD LIST★

- ☆ Shrimp cocktail
- ☆ Fresh fruit
- ☆ Crudités (pronounced crew-dee-tay) (fancy way of saying raw veggies and dip)
- ☆ Cheese and crackers
- ☆ Sushi
- ☆ Chicken wings
- ☆ Green salad
- ☆ Dinner rolls
- ☆ Steak

- ☆ Baked salmon
- ☆ Chicken à l'orange (fancy way of saying chicken with orange sauce)
- ☆ Pasta primavera (fancy way of saying noodles with vegetables)
- ☆ Potatoes au gratin (rhymes with rotten, but it's actually good) (fancy way of saying potatoes with cheesy sauce)
- ☆ Vegetable medley (fancy way of saying mixed veggies)

Then, just when I thought I couldn't take another bite, they brought out the DESSERTS!

Monica's fave

My fave

Anyhow, Monica was feeling the same way I was after all that food, so she's going to wait a little while before she makes her final decision. I'm sure whatever she chooses to serve at the wedding will be D-LISH!

Well, I hope I can manage to roll myself into bed. Nighty-night, Diary.

5:21 a.m.

It's time to rise and shine, dear Diary!

Why am I awake while the rest of the world is in snoozeland? Because today is Monica's shower!—and I have tons to do. Wish me luck!

10:18 p.m.

Well, everyone said the food was D-licious, the games were D-lightful, and the decorations were D best! Even my kitty-cat, Ginger, said it was PURR-fect!

Well, almost perfect—
except for when Christie
broke out in hives!

Do they call them
hives because it looks
like you got stung by
a bunch of bees?

Here's the scoop: I decorated the
house with yellow carnations because Monica
loves yellow flowers. What we didn't know was
that Christie is allergic to carnations! Change
of plans. Now the bridesmaids will carry lilies
instead of carnations at the wedding. PHEW!
Good thing we found out now.

The shower was neat, but I am
BEAT! YAAAWN. Good night, Diary.

10:42 p.m.

P.S. Today, Monica gave Skipper the song
she wants her to sing at the wedding. But
Skipper is still too nervous!
What a D-lemma! Well, good night.

Dear Diary,

Today was gr8! Here's why:

Mary, Skipper, and I were driving to the mall today to buy wedding gifts for Monica & Robert.

What 2 get for Monica and Robert

♥ **Toaster**

no way! 2 boring!

♥ **Television**

Hope they don't fight over the remote control!

♥ **Towels**

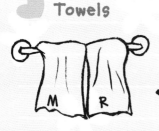

no way! 2 boring!

♥ **Tent**

What's with all the Ts????

♥ **Tiki Torches**

J/K (just kidding)

So we're walking in the mall, and all of a sudden I hear Mary and Skipper singing that new song by Isabel Moore— and they sound AWESOME! I never knew that Mary had such a nice singing voice. And then it came to me! I may just have the perfect idea. But I have to run it by Monica first. I'll keep you posted. TTFN, Diary!

Dear Diary,

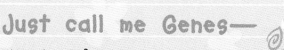

Just call me Genes—

that's short for genius.

Bona Fide Genius

After hearing Mary and Skipper sing,
I asked Monica what she thought about
them doing **a duet** at the wedding.

POSSIBLE ANSWERS

    a. No way!

    b. Maybe

    c. Gr8 idea!

    d. Absolute-o-mundo!

Monica said d. Absolute-o-mundo!

When I asked Skipper, she chose c. Then she gave me a big hug and said I was the best sister EVER!

World's Best Sister

Then I called Mary and she said YES!

So everything is settled. Monica will have not one but two singers at her wedding, Skipper won't be nervous, and Mary gets to be a part of the wedding! PHEW! All this genius stuff is exhausting. I'm wiped!

Good night, Diary.

Dear Diary,

I went back to the mall again today. **Here's the good news:** I finally thought of the perfect gift for Monica and Robert. You know how they love being outside? And everyone has to eat. So put the two together and VOILÀ! (That's French for TA-DA.) I'm going to get them **a picnic backpack**—with plates, glasses, silverware, and a plaid blanket for two. They can use it on their honeymoon. They're taking a bicycling trip through France! Doesn't that sound **très bien?** (That's French for **really cool.**)

Now for the bad news: The store was all sold out of the picnic backpacks! But they should have some later this week. And now for the really really bad news: I HAVE TO GO BACK TO THE MALL AGAIN! Wow! Never thought I'd complain about shopping! Maybe I'd better go see a doctor.

RX—Prescription

SHOPICILLIN to cure a bad case of mall-o-phobia.

Take two and go shopping in the morning.

Dr. DooLots

Au revoir (that's French for catch you later), Diary.

Ladies and Gentlemen (and Diaries),

The WEDDING COUNTDOWN has begun.
(10) 9 8 7 6 5 4 3 2 1 MORE DAYS!

Well, I saved the day again. (Okay, actually it was Ken who saved the day, but, you know . . .)

So here's the scoop: Robert was playing softball yesterday and **he sprained his ankle** sliding into home plate! Don't worry. He'll be okay in time for the wedding.

But the thing is, Monica and Robert have been taking ballroom dancing lessons so they can dance to their first song.

Luckily, they only had one lesson left, but
Monica needed to learn this fancy-schmantzy spin.
So I called Ken to see if he could fill in. He said,
"No pro-blemo!" Isn't he the BEST?!!

Night-night, Diary.

Dear Diary,

⑥ 5 4 3 2 1 MORE DAYS
TILL THE WEDDING!

I think I ran another marathon today, and I still have lots to do before the **BIG DAY!** Plus, **my tootsies are killing me!** Here's why: I went to the shoe store and picked up my **turquoise** high heels that match my **turquoise** dress. Then I thought I should break in my shoes so they'd be comfortable on the day of the wedding. **Big mistake!**

FLOWER POWER

bought rose petals for Kelly's flower girl basket

STEP ON IT

picked up shoes here

dropped off bride-and-groom topper for wedding cake

PIECE OF CAKE

met Ken
for lunch

CAFÉ
CAFÉ

CREATIVE
CARDS

Congratulations!

found perfect
wedding card to
go with perfect
wedding gift

picked up
Kelly's flower
girl dress—
SO CUTE!

THE
LITTLE
PRINCESS

So you get the picture. The good news: my shoes
are completely broken in now. **The bad news:
I may never be able to walk again.**
Maybe Monica will let me wear my slippers to the
wedding?

Hope I can hobble over to my bed, because these
feet R beat. Good night, Diary. Sweet feet
dreams.

11:37 p.m.

On a busy scale of 1 to 10, **today was a 9.8.** Just imagine what tomorrow is going to be like!!! Monica, Kira, Christie, and I all got manicures and facials at the beauty salon. And in case you were wondering, **my feet have recovered.**

The rehearsal went smoothly. Skipper and Mary sang a little bit of their duet and they sounded gr8! And then, as if the day wasn't perfect enough, Monica gave all of us bridesmaid gifts—pretty strands of pearls and matching pearl earrings. Isn't she the BEST?!

I'm so excited about tomorrow! I hope I'll be able to fall asleep. Wish me luck!

12:14 a.m.

Still awake. Maybe if I count sheep. One, two, three . . .

12:43 a.m.

Okay, the sheep aren't working. Too loud. Let's try kittens. One, two . . .

YAAAWN. Good night, Diary.

Dear Diary,

Well, Robert and Monica are finally MARRIED! Everyone had a fab time!

Monica looked gorgeous in her white wedding dress and veil. And Skipper and Mary's duet was so amazing that everyone cheered for them at the end. The bride and groom's first dance was perfect **(thanks again, Ken)**. Then the Blue Beats started to play (YES!) and it was PARTY TIME!

The food was D-LISH, especially the four-tiered coconut wedding cake. And before I knew it, Monica threw her bouquet—and Kira caught it!

I don't think I've ever been more tired in my whole entire life! YAAAAAAWN.

Good night, Diary.

Dear Diary,

Helping Monica plan her wedding was **tons-o-work but tons-o-fun.** I know Monica and Robert will **remember their special day forever.** And I can look back at this diary anytime I want and remember **all the funny, happy, crazy times** we had. When I get married (someday????), I hope I'll have as much fun sharing my wedding day with my family and friends.

C U L8-ER, DIARY!

Love,
Barbie

Who will I marry?

What is your dream wedding?
Write about it here.

Barbie™

Here are some great Barbie™ storybooks to collect!

PASSPORT SERIES

BARBIE RULES SERIES

HORSESHOE CLUB SERIES

GIRLS CLUB SERIES

MAGNET LOOK-LOOKS

STEP INTO READING